Oh Where, Oh Where, Can The Letter Z Be?

By Allison C. Hefner

alo
PUBLISHING
INTERNATIONAL

ISBN: 978-1-61244-728-5
Library of Congress Control Number: 2019940878

Printed in the United States of America

Halo Publishing International
1100 NW Loop 410
Suite 700 - 176
San Antonio, Texas 78213
www.halopublishing.com
contact@halopublishing.com

To Michael and Ethan, may this book inspire you to pen your own stories one day as you have inspired me. And to children everywhere: we should all be celebrated for who we are and for our unique place in this world.

Something strange has happened to the alphabet. I just don't know how upset to get! What happened to the letter Z? Oh where, oh where, can he be?

Why it was just two days ago before my heart was filled with woe. I went to practice my ABCs, only to find that he was missing: the letter Z.

8

I was reading and practicing with all my might, when, all of a sudden, I was overcome with fright! The letter Z was gone without a trace, and there wasn't a single letter to stand in his place.

Oh my, oh my! There was nothing behind the letter Y! I blinked and then rubbed my eye, and ever so softly, I began to cry. The alphabet was no longer complete. Without Z there, it just wasn't as neat.

I know he must be sad, or maybe even aghast, to always have to be standing last. It must be a very difficult thing to face, always coming in the final place.

But every letter is special, and if I could just tell him, why, maybe he wouldn't have had to fly. Now that he's decided to cut and run, the alphabet just isn't as fun.

Oh where, oh where can the letter Z be?

Perhaps he's on the beach drinking lemonade. Could he be trying to get lost in a parade? Maybe he thinks that he belongs somewhere else, like as a part of a number line or hidden in a book on the shelf. Could he be spending time with some sheep, helping a child to get to sleep?

Where are you, silly old Z? It surely isn't better than being with your family!

Oh, Z! Can't you see? Everyone has their place in this world, every boy and every girl. The same is true for every letter. With all 26, the alphabet is so much better.

How else would we spell such amazing words, like pizza and zip? And without Z, dazzle doesn't even sound hip.

So, if you can hear me Z, I think you should know, there really wasn't a good reason for you to go. Let's get the alphabet back on track! Please, oh please, Z, come immediately back!

Because there is no one else like you, and there never will be a replacement for the wonderful letter Z. You are special, unique, and one of a kind, a letter unlike any other, a rare find.

So, come back, come back, wherever you might be. And shine brightly in your spot, like the star you are, Z.

Wait, just a minute. . . what is that? Did I see that the letter Z came back? He must have heard me! He must have known just how amazing he is and that he never should have flown.

Thank you, Z, for coming home! Be proud of who you are, and know that you're never alone. You've got 25 letters supporting you with pride, plus millions and millions of friends and readers worldwide.

Hooray! Hooray! I just don't know how much happier I can get! Z is back, and he's the perfect ending to the alphabet!

CPSIA information can be obtained
at www.ICGtesting.com
Printed in the USA
BVHW061604261119
564447BV00013B/160/P